THE BURIAL

Dean Drinkel

To My Lovey, And Special Friend Kate. A.E.

From, The King Of Madness.

MINERVA PRESS
MONTREUX LONDON WASHINGTON

Dec 31 1995.

THE BURIAL
Copyright © Dean Drinkel 1995

All Rights Reserved

ISBN 1 85863 387 7

First published 1995 by
MINERVA PRESS
1 Cromwell Place
London SW7 2JE

Printed in Great Britain by
B.W.D. Ltd., Northolt, Middlesex.

THE BURIAL

ABOUT THE AUTHOR

Dean Drinkel was born in Farnham, Surrey, in 1972, and was educated in West london. Having published over twenty short stories, he is currently working on a second collection of stories, a comic book/graphic novel, and is preparing background research for his first novel.

Contrary to popular belief, he is not mad.

ACKNOWLEDGMENTS: In Memorium

In the dark of the night, the audience sat in their seats, very patiently. They knew that they shouldn't have been there at all but, what the hell. No-one came down this side of the City anymore. No-one still living, at least.

The small theatre had seen better days, as had its current inhabitants. The once plush, red velvet seats were now aged and rotten. All kinds of creatures lived therein and ensured that they enjoyed whatever morsels they had to offer.

There was quite a crowd tonight. It wasn't anything particularly out of the ordinary, but some had decided to get off their rear ends for once and make the trip across the spectral plane. This meant that there were many new faces in the Cinema tonight; a few musicians, the odd actor or two and, others of that ilk known as the Entertainment Industry.

One of these bystanders stood out. He wore nothing save a pair of blood stained jeans and white sneakers. What he was doing here, no-one was quite sure, but they all stared at his headless corpse. Where his cranium should have been was just a mass of red tissue and a selection of hair strands.

The same question was on the tip of the onlookers' tongues. How was he to view the proceedings?

A man came onto the stage. He was smartly dressed but it was a damn shame that those knife marks had expanded over the years. They had quite ruined the Armani Suit.

"Can I have everyone's attention?" he asked, and everyone stopped talking and looked in his direction. Except, of course, the headless man. He started to tap the floor and the chairs in front of him, much to the annoyance of everyone concerned.

The Compere was pissedoff at this and rightly so. He pulled out an ancient pistol and filled the nuisance full of lead balls. It worked; the man with no head stopped what he was doing and put his hands to the mass above his neck, created a strange and macabre mouth out of the rotten flesh, and mumbled, "Sorry."

"Right," said the man on the stage. "That's better. Just before we begin, Ladies and Gentlemen, there are a few people I would like to thank."

The audience waited...
"Okay, here goes:

To: Joseph M., Michael S., Mike M., Bill B., Peter B., Madonna Ciccone, my Mother, Father, Nigel and Simon. My close family and friends; including, Sarah, Rachael, Julie, Steve, St. John, William, Roger, Gina, Tom, Colin, Jayne D., Jenny, Martin F., Wil Wheaton and Justin.

And finally, an extra special thanks to my "Tutors", without them, maybe what follows would never have happened: Clive Barker, Stephen King and James Herbert. To those I missed, catch you next time.

Love to you all."

They sat there in silence. What was he going on about? They watched as he stepped off the stage and a voice came across the Auditorium, "On with the show..."

JUNE 1994

vii

CONTENTS

Page

WEIRD

Inanotherbangbloodscreamssilencenothing

Here, I am different. My eyes hang wildly and I can see petals fall from the skyscrapers in the distance.

It is true. I am among the dead.

On this side we are all equal; dead meat and depleted spirits.

I blink and there is a creature dancing above my head. I have broken my neck so I can't see my body, but I can feel the blood flow from several wounds. I can't move, yet in some perverted sense I think I am happy.

This creature!

It is transparent but I know it. I see what it sees, feel what it feels.

It is there now, just hovering above me. Its wide eyes just peer into the distance laughing at my destruction. I know it longs to be there because I long to be there.

Somehow I am his prisoner, he is my gaoler.

A spiral tries to engulf me and I try to remember that night. I remember walking into the shop. I look at the bread; I pick up a white loaf. I feel something over my shoulder. And...

And.

And.

And...?

Nothing...

The spiral bites at my legs and I fall...

Something wet hits me and I see the creature in all its glory.

I ask it, "Who are you?"

It flew into the air, screaming and wailing. Its long white hair trailing behind it like a comet: a Supa Nova.

I grow sick of the change in tenses. Here Past is Present and Present is Future.

It screams at me, "I AM DEATH! I AM THE SHATTERER OF WORLDS! I AM AN ANGEL OF DARKNESS!"

The words are hailed through the heavens.

"STOP IT!" I plead.

"Why?" it quietly whispered, again only feet from my face.

"Because you mock me."

"Isn't that the point of man? To mock the gods?" And Time was gone.

My head is hurting. I used to run my fingers through my blond hair but now all I feel is metal on top of my skull.

The blood begins to gush for a little time and then all of a sudden I feel invisible hands plug the wound with hot mud, which makes me laugh. For a little while at least...

I can't remember my name.

Is it Ken?

Joseph?

James?

Sarah?

What?

WHY CAN'T I REMEMBER?

"Because you aren't supposed to."

These words hit me like a breath of fresh air. There is something else out there. It wasn't just my imagination!

For the hell of it, an old film is run in front of my vision, but one of my eyes becomes all misty and I can only see one half of it.

It wasn't much fun anyway, just someone being shot in a supermarket, although I did laugh when the killer sat down with his victim's head in his hands and he began to drink his blood.

Poor Man.

I opened my one good eye. Those buildings were gone, replaced by a red hue which was moving closer towards me.

And a sound.

A beating.

Drums. A tattoo.

"Breath."

I wondered who had spoken. It was a new presence. Different from the creature before, but yet something equal.

As it pulsed before me it was blue when it spoke.

"Speak not. We will soon be travelling."

"Answer me one thing."

"Speak!"

"My name. What is it?"

Silence. Then...

"Your name is Gary."

"Oh."

"Prepare Yourself."

I felt a harsh jab in my stomach and I was sure that something was being pumped into me. A fluid. Harder and harder. I need to scream. Long to scream, but my mouth refuses to open.

Through the slits of my eyes I could see I was covered in a thin white film. I was floating! I lifted my eyes to my face. I was whole again. THANKS BE TO GOD.

Horror floods my brain...

"What's going on?"

"You're going back."

"But..." Now I feel so tired.

Silence, I can't fight it anymore.

I closed my eyes and the blackness chilled me.

The drumming was louder, thumping skull. The ghost had left me and I was a stranger, even to myself.

I knew everything. I had seen myself. My soul had never left me.

Now what did He say my name was?

I knew... and the suspension broke. I wasn't floating anymore... but flooded by water, blinded by the purest of white light.

And I awoke.

"Mrs. Shaw, it's a beautiful baby boy!"

OPERATA

The battle was over. The carrion birds screamed in delight as they picked at the wounds, fed on the ocean of flesh that lay before them.

Lying there, amongst the throng, he knew that he was a part of history. It had been written: men had come and men had gone, preaching their word and retelling the future. Like the black flower concealed within the wild honeysuckle bush. Civilization had been offered to the warring legends, rejected by most.

The sounds of death, like the armies before them had given up the ghost, waiting for the scavengers to take them elsewhere. Beyond this desolation lay a yellowish mist which had been vomited from the bowels of the earth and now hung like a heavy curtain. Even the Drum, that had only hours before been heard throughout the hills beating its Cry, was, like its master, pierced and silent among the macabre throng.

The elements were upset however, because there was a survivor. He had been revived by the blazing sun which now scorched his open wounds. Dividing the outlandish material from atop his weary body he tried to sit up. He rubbed the sands of time from his face, cleansing his soul of death, the glory, the religion that he had been a part of and to some extent, the cause of.

There was a cry from the hills and the warrior tried to move his legs, but they lay trapped under the dual weight of guilt and reason. Wincing, he let his upper body fall back into place and screamed into the silence.

Outburst followed outburst and these acted like a magical spell, a hex, or chant, because in the distance the mist began to part, and Death's speech to his new disciples was replaced by harmonic singing - angelic voices in Hell's territory.

He tried to stir once again and repeated his attempt to stand. He pushed some of the discarded masonry under his head and upper torso so that at the very least he could stay sitting up and see the wonder. He squinted into the mêlée and there, like a fantasy, were three women. Travelling quickly they covered the vast distance in a short time and to him and his weary eyes it seemed like they were laughing, nay orgasming, over the carnage that lay beneath them.

The warrior cried.

These beings were probably the most beautiful creatures he had ever seen. Better by far than the females of his own kind and even God himself would savour women such as these.

Time was endless and they floated closer to him. They stopped their merriment and the one with red hair whispered something into a horn which she took from her belt. The garbage that covered the field: weapons, helmets, bones and such like blew away, floating in the air with her voice and was lost in all dimensions. The black haired female spoke to the man: "Hail Boothka! From substance we are called. You are chosen as we are chosen. Accept your destiny."

Their voices were just as beautiful. Perfection.

The third commanded him, "Accept, or be dammed until the tides of time are no more. Have you nothing to say, Boothka?"

"I am Magus to the Kingdom of Carthage. I know no Boothka."

Redhair spoke again.

"The Prophet foretold in the Book of Mother that 'The one named Boothka would survive the war to end all wars, forever to be known as the War of Heresy and claim himself also to be Prophet.'"

Magus replied, "It is God's will that I have survived but I am no prophet."

The three communicated telepathically like the Old Ones and then the third spoke in a voice that shook the heavens.

"We are the Badhbh, the Macha and the Morrighan: Judge, Jury and Execution. As you have so far refused to accept your destiny we will in turn show you things that have never been shown to mortal eyes. Accept this or you will never see the setting of another sun!"

Sensations returned back to his body and the warrior stood up. Dusting himself down and removing the armour from his body he smiled at the women, naked.

"Show me," he said.

The three women laughed.

"First, the Badhbh."

It was a ceremony.

There were many, speaking as one.

The warrior was sitting in the centre of a great circle. There was a fire in the distance, but he didn't feel the heat. He looked around at the surrounding group, however there was too much smoke to make any one face recognisable.

There was chanting which was now reaching a level of audibility that was near to breaking point. Sweat began to leak down his face, his back, his legs, when he noticed that blood was pouring from his hands and feet, staining the grass beneath him.

The chanting ceased and all was silent but he could still hear the noise inside him, trapped there like a part of him.

The smoke cleared revealing a great totem with a white bird sitting on top. The yellow light from the fire dazzled his eyes and the bird spoke: "This is not for your kind."

The warrior closed his eyes and, ignoring the pain from his wounds, continued with the music.

He heard the flapping of wings as the bird flew away, leaving the totem to crumble in a pile of dust. In his mind's eye, he saw the fire snuffed out by a black unicorn which had appeared from behind the mountains.

The silent natives resumed with their chanting and began to rock backwards and forwards as if knowing and the warrior was sure that in the embers of the dying embers of the fire he could see three monkeys, mocking him.

One by one the chanters pulled from their costumes great gold daggers, and while still chanting they stood and turned to one another. And then, in one great swoop they stabbed each other, falling to the ground, consumed by the dust the totem had left.

The warrior, against the orders of the bird, opened his eyes ready to call out, to scream, when he noticed there was no fire, no death; there were no chanters! He was back where it all started.

He looked at his hands. There were still traces of blood in his hands.

The Badhbh walked forward and offered him the white bird in a small silver cage. The warrior made ready to accept the gift when she opened her hands revealing a beating heart, recently plucked from one of God's creatures.

The warrior screamed as the heart was handed to him and a voice from deep inside of him whispered, "And now, the Macha."

He was in some kind of temple. A temple that lay at the bottom of a great hill. Everything around him lay in desolation. Tables and chairs were uprooted and behind him a velvet curtain that had once covered the golden altar, now hung ripped from its wooden rail. Even the Great Book was unread, torn and shred.

Under one of the vacant windows, an inscription was written on the wall in charcoal. It was in Roman and read, "De Mortuis nil nisi bonum."

The warrior traced his fingers along the words, feeling each letter slowly and surely, remembering the past, knowing the future.

He left the temple and looked up at the summit of the hill. There was the mark of the long dead Empire: the Crucifixion. The warrior traced his way up the winding path, ignoring the crows, ignoring the skulls. He turned and stared at the distance he had come. The town, like the Empire, was dead.

There was movement behind him and the warrior faced the top of the hill. Sitting beneath one of the crosses was a man. It was strange that he hadn't seen him before!

The Magus walked up to the man, who was wearing a remnant of the curtain that hung in the temple. The stranger was cross-legged and his head and face was hidden in the velvet cloth. The warrior sat opposite him and waited several seconds before speaking.

"Who are you?" he asked.

"Ecce Homo!" the man replied.

"That language died centuries ago. Who are you?" the warrior repeated.

"Obiit," the hooded man said, pointing to the cross.

"Who died? Where am I?" the warrior asked. He stood up, adrenaline flowing, panicking, his heart beating loudly in his head.

Then the warrior realised.

"I don't want to know. Leave me alone! Please! I thought... "

The other pointed to the heavens, then the cross, then revealing his face to the warrior.

"You thought what? That it was all fiction! A story to rock little children to sleep?"

Then he added, more softly, "It was real. All of it was real. But now no-one believes, they have no heart."

The warrior fell to his knees and looked deeply into the eyes of the stranger.

"Vox populi, vox Dei," the warrior whispered.

"The people? They have no voice. That died with their Lord."

"I think I have something for you," the warrior said.

He opened his hand, revealing the beating heart. He offered it to the stranger who took it and placed it in his tunic. As their hands touched it was if the warrior knew the world, knew everything there was to know.

He watched as the stranger stood up and walked away. The man stopped after several paces and strolled back to the warrior, placed a hand on his shoulder and whispered, "Peccavi. Peccavi."

As the son of man resumed his walk, the warrior touched the cross, closed his eyes and waited. In his mind he saw the white bird and it spoke to him.

"It was the Morrighan. It was the Morrighan."

It was at that instance that he understood everything. He ran after the stranger, never knowing if he was going to reach him, but nonetheless still running.

When the sun rose over the hill, it was the start of a new day. The mark of a new age. The heart of the people had been returned to them.

And it was on that day, that another man came into the temple and began to sweep away the desolation that had lain there for many eons. And he was followed by another, and another and so on.

And a day came to pass that they destroyed the temple, levelled the hill, burnt the crosses and built themselves a new town with its own inscription. The inscription that reads, "Sic transit gloria mundi."

So passes the glory of the world.

Operata.

THE RED HAVEN

Things had been done to him as a child that he didn't want to remember. The only good recollection he had was that of the Haven. It was a strange kind of place. A dusty track here, a dirty track there, he had walked those streets for a long time.

There was no sun, but it wasn't dark. Dead birds lay by the roadside. Many looked devoid of souls and all had died a most horrible death. The place was without life except for the shadows. Now they had life. They were everywhere; in the trees, in the fields. He felt turned inside out and imagined that he was looking at his own innards.

"What a place to be taken as a child!" he thought, and returned to his normal state. He had no choice but to continue playing with the knife until his mother told him it was time for tea. But even when he sat at the table eating his burgers, he was unable to forget the redness of it all.

There was nothing to do but grow up.

Bugs. There were bugs everywhere! And he felt guilty. He waved as he watched his girlfriend - ex-girlfriend - fall from the window.

So that was that, he thought, and went back inside.

He walked the streets. Hands in pockets, collar up, hat down. He felt like Philip Marlowe, as he kicked the odd bottle or Coke can. Here he was, senseless, at his wits' end. Breathing. Living. He had seen people die before, it was his profession. So what was wrong with him? He played with a match in his mouth, rolling it across from one side to the other, using his lips, using his breath.

Later, the glass doors opened.

An object circled his head as he stood by the elevator.

"Mr. Hodes. Nice to see you early sir!"

He hit it then whispered, "Yes, a change is as good as a rest."

The office was empty, fitting somehow, because this was to be his final day. He opened his drawer, saw the dead rat, and put that with the rest of his things into the carrier bag. Minutes later and he was standing outside.

The first chapter of his life was over.

He thought of the Red Haven.

He didn't love much, but he revelled in playing the oddball. Tonight was to be no different. He had been sitting in the bar for about an hour before the crowd came in. It was an office party and a large group such as this had another bonus: he had the chance to disappear.

Within minutes he was invited into the throng and joined in wholeheartedly, and they laughed as he did his rendition of Milton with a pint of lager on his head. Soon, however, he began to feel the effects of the drink and, mixed with the flashing blue strobe, he lay slumped on the floor, dribble spilling forth from his mouth, half-empty glass in his hand.

He felt it rain in his mind and inside the pub. There were soft drips to begin with, but then it fell harder and harder. He wiped it from his face and watched while the others danced. Sitting up, he shuddered as there was a crack of thunder, a flash of lightning.

As he stared at himself, he pulled his Mac tighter around his neck and reluctantly put up his umbrella. It was strange because this was the first recollection he had of it raining in the desert. Dryness was the king of this land, the sun so unbearably hot. His friend William waved as he rode on the back of a camel. There was no choice but to get up off of the floor and thumb a lift.

The strobe lay broken. One of the revellers had thrown something at it. Hodes gingerly stood up. The barman was standing on a ladder trying to fix it, but to no avail. The landlady came out from the back with a chorus of catcalls which really riled the barman. She put out some sandwiches and a birthday cake which was quickly gobbled up. James - or was it Peter? - was pouring a drink over his head. There was some noise from the corner, a woman screamed, and he saw some strange kind of animal smashing his head against the wall.

Hodes remembered his girlfriend, and their trips to the Red Haven. Her name was Mandy Gabriel. Before they scooped her off the concrete she had been really pretty. She was damn near perfect, even her light brown hair caught the sunlight like no other colour could even imitate. The problem was however, that he didn't respect her. She had wanted to see the Red Haven, and even though he had refused at first, she kept nagging him and nagging him, until there was no choice. She wanted to see it so he showed her. No subtlety to it. No slow motion. In at the deep-end.

William soon came back into view. The rain had died. It was far easier to walk in the sand. William jumped off the animal, gave some money to the slave. And he walked over.

"Jonathan Hodes. How are you, my old chap? How is the book?"

"It's finished."

"Already?"

"No... not completed. Finished."

"What are you rambling on about old man?"

"I'm burnt out. I'm trying to please too many people and I'm forgetting about myself. Words scare me."

"I'm not listening to this Hodes. I want that book in a few days. Visit the Red Haven or whatever it is you call it. There's a lot of money riding on this one."

Hodes fell asleep. There wasn't much else to say or do. But he licked his lips and tasted his dream.

The whole country comes to a standstill when it snows. Trains, buses, cars. Nothing moves. The ice, the slush, the cold.

He had been moved. From his window he could see man's eternal struggle. He laughed to himself. He felt an itch on his nose and longed to relieve himself but he couldn't because his hands were tied.

He had come to a decision however, that the time was right. When the woman returned and loosened his bonds he took a chunk out of her arm. And when he tasted her flesh, and deeper still, her blood, he was transported to the Red Haven as a child. This time, forever.

FRIENDS OF MOTHER

When we were younger, mother used to have some very strange people over to stay. In other times, other books, they would have been called "by-blows". But my sisters and I just called them "Friends of Mother". They were amazing little creatures and would do anything you wanted them to do. They would skip, jump, play dead. You could play hide and seek, knock-knock, pom pom one-two-three, and then, when it was time to go, they'd say good-bye and promise to come and play next holiday.

The years passed and the "Friends of Mother" came to see us every summer holiday. Mother enjoyed their company - while some played with us the rest helped Mother with her cooking, her knitting, her washing. Not having a father around - he died during the war - could have hampered both her's and our progress. But it never did. At an early age I began to read books. Anything I could get my hands on; Camus, Kazantzakis, Maturin. Only the best. And naturally, as my reading diversified and matured, so did my writing, until I was naturally superior. It was about this time - my fourteenth, fifteenth birthday - that I realised that the "Friends" didn't seem as big in number as before. They always seemed to vanish when you wanted them. As if they were plotting something. I'm not too sure whether Mother consented to their behaviour, considering that they were her friends, her guests. But what was she to do?

I was studying hard. I was writing a thesis on the Gothic poets when I felt a wooden tap on my shoulder. I turned around swiftly. I do not like being disturbed when I'm working and I have on numerous occasions told them so. Standing there was one of the now tiresome creatures, a little more disfigured than the rest.

"Well, what is it?" I asked harshly.

"Would you please come with me. We have something to show you."

It shifted away without reply.

I threw down my pen in disgust. The muse had quite gone. I was alone, my sisters had gone to University in Oxford a long time since, and my mother was shopping in town for some jumpers.

"Where are you taking me?" I shouted, stepping after it, careful not to slip in the trail of mucus. It was this, for some strange reason, that reminded me of my sisters. We had grown quite apart, too many motions. They compared me to Confucius, I compared them to Blyton. We liked each other, but their existences were far, far behind mine.

With reservations I left the comfort of my bedroom, the place I hold so dear. Within a few blurred minutes (had we really travelled that fast?) we were somewhere. Somewhere I hadn't been in a very long time, somewhere I had forgotten. The basement of my past: the cellar. There they all were - all the "Friends". They were surrounding something. It was moving, real; some kind of monster. I moved closer. Astonished. Wondering. All the little creatures were joined together, unifying, an unnatural union. But there was something wicked, something I knew, about the union. Mother's rings. It spoke.

"Come Geraldine! Join our club! Ultimate knowledge."

The room was heaving, nay breathing, hot as a furnace. I wanted to leave but I wanted to stay, if only for the knowing. I sat down on the edge of the step, and let their tentacles flick over my body, exciting my pleasures. I was joining in, my skin was being rubbed, and felt rubbery, elastic; my bones broke into thousands of tiny fragments. I felt like melted plastic, a river of blood, bile, existence.

As more and more creatures expanded with me, moved on me, around me, I began to feel the consciousness of others. I suppose they could be called other victims, but that was too harsh a term. I was really enjoying the moment, a victory for literature - an artist's crescendo. My spinal cord finally gave way and I splatted onto the floor, cold against the warm cement. We-I-It, began to move, slide along. So much for Jung's 'Collective consciousness' I thought! Or was it Marx? Durkheim? I couldn't remember.

Only one of my eyes was left to exist, its stalk stood high above the endless mass. I looked above me. There - spread-eagled, from the ceiling, in chains - were my sisters. There wasn't that much left of them, most of their innards had already been consumed. I looked away and wondered where we were heading. I moved my eye a little to the left. Ah, there: the prize! The drains. Two hands appeared, lifted the cover up and threw it to the side. Thousands of little mouths appeared and as my eye was slowly swallowed I could hear the laughing.

Oh the laughing...

THE VISITOR

I awoke with the whole of my right side hurting. I sat up, turned the light on, and pulled the covers back. There was a smallish lump on the inside of my thigh. I was amazed that such a little thing could hurt so much. I scratched and pulled, prodded and fondled the hard lump, but to no avail. So after a little while I went into the bathroom, found some aspirin and returned swiftly to my bed.

I couldn't believe my luck. Within a few minutes most of the pain had gone. The lump was still there and it was slightly red, but I was sure that some of the hardness had gone down.

It was dark. I must have switched the light off and gone back to sleep. It was still night-time but I thought that it would be morning soon because I could hear the singing of the birds outside the window. And then I heard it.

"Simon."

My name. I went to turn the light on, but I stopped, because I was scared. Hang on, it couldn't be a burglar because the voice knew my name. My heart slowed down a little.

"Simon!" It was now a little louder, but still somehow muffled. I pulled back the cover and in the morning light I saw my leg. I switched on the bedside lamp.

I had previously forgotten all about that lump. And how it had changed. It was much larger and covered most of my thigh and now there was a slit that went from one side of my leg to the other. It was strange because I couldn't feel it.

And then the slit moved, and seemed to smile and again spoke my name, "Hello Simon. Nice to meet you!"

APPLES IN MY EYES

The man who claimed to be God cried into his hourglass, but no-one in the room cared.

The snow had been washed clean away. The country returned to normality. But what she had said still hurt his feelings. There was no doubting that. He looked at the unopened presents that lay side-by-side with the uprooted tree and he tried to remember what she had smelt like because for some strange reason he had forgotten.

The clasp on the cabinet was too easily broken. She had taken the key with her because she said that she didn't trust him. What a silly woman, as if! He played with the weapon, loaded as usual, and then fell onto the couch and slept.

He soon got bored with sleeping and when he awoke he decided that it would be a good idea to go for a walk. Within minutes he was walking through places unknown. All around him there were fauna and flora, something that he was quite unfamiliar with. He bent down and smelt the yellow flowers that were hanging over, onto the dusty track. For reasons best known only to himself, he took a decoration from his pocket and perched it on the end of a broken willow branch.

He had never been in this part of the country before. But there were certain things that he recognised. He could hear a bell ringing up ahead, and he knew that this was the place for him. He began to run but once it rained he began to slip and slide in the undergrowth. But even that wasn't going to stop him reaching his destination. That was the place for him. He needed it and it needed him.

After a while he began to catch sight of it.

The birds had stopped singing and even the flowers were painting in the opposite direction. That bell-noise was getting louder and louder and was beginning to play havoc with his head, his senses, but still he carried on, ignoring his pain, mimicking the beat with his teeth.

He stopped in his tracks. The building had crept up on him before he had had the time to reach it, but he was glad that he was here all the same. The bell had stopped ringing but for the first time he had caught sight of it, suspended in the yellow tower.

In front of him was a big gate which sliced the sand-dunes in half. There were many footprints that led up to the gate, which for some reason he placed his own feet, as if in ritual. After a few steps he veered off to the left and walked through a little black door.

Inside the room that had mirrors on every wall was a little pot-bellied dwarf that slapped his naked stomach as if in unison with the bell that had fallen silent. The dwarf rolled his pyramid.

The paintings...

"So what do you think of these?" He pointed skywards. "I had them done yesterday, but I'm not too sure if they fit in with the general... ah, you know! Please sit." He slapped his stomach a few more times and pulled on his belly button, which was rather large, even for a dwarf.

"Ahum. I am sorry. I don't even know where I am. But I will admit that your etchings are rather fetching."

"Don't be so melodramatic! Either you like them or you don't!" said the dwarf, then added, "Just say so. It's the same with your writings. No-one knows if they are coming or going!"

"You what? Do you know me?"

"Of course. Everyone knows who you are - Clark Temple, bit part writer, large part junkie."

"Hey you! I've never taken one drug in my life!"

"Can you prove it? And anyway, you must have done something because no sane person could write the stuff you do!"

"Yeah. Well. Who the hell are you?"

"I'm Potbelly. I'm in charge around here. My blue shirt is here somewhere, and I could prove it."

"Where am I?"

"Somewhere and nowhere. So tell me "Clarky", why do you write about blood and guts anyway?"

"Because I can't write about anything else. Torture comes easily to me. I despise stories with happy endings. I always want to see the hero lose a limb or two."

"This is so sad. A nice lad like you. You should be getting drunk and writing about nice summer days, warm winter nights. You know the kind of thing."

"I can't do that. Anyway people like what I do."

"That may be so. But some people also hate it and hate you for it. Only last year I had several people in here complaining that you were depressing the hell out of them. They were close to suicide until I showed them another alternative."

"And what was that?"

"To be you."

"What do you mean?"

"The voices.... but that is all I'm going to say on the matter."

The dwarf floated out of the room. Temple went to follow but the door had gone. He returned his attention to the pyramid and there was a gleaming new black typewriter with one piece of brilliant white paper rearing its ugly head. Temple sat down cross-legged and began to type...

THE MAN WHO CLAIMED TO BE GOD CRIED INTO HIS HOURGLASS BUT NO-ONE IN THE ROOM CARED...

He looked up at the etchings but because the top of the ceiling was too far up he could only imagine what was drawn there: fallen angels, sacred Madonnas. But it was all too much and he began to shout and run around the room, beating the mirrors, beating himself.

He fell to his knees.

"Leave me alone! I want to be normal! I don't want to be melodramatic! I want people to love my work! I want people to read my writings!"

He beat the floor. And had an idea. He forced the paper up a few lines with his hands and began to type. As his fingers raped the machine he swore that out of the corner of his eye he could see all kinds of people, or kinds of monsters escape making faces at him and finally escaping out of the room. He licked his lips. He liked his first line and lapped at his sweat.

THE SUN BEAT DOWN UPON LUCY'S BRONZE BODY AND SHE SHIVERED AS DAVID RUBBED THE SUNCREAM IN...

Yes. I'm almost there. This is it.

But when the dwarf came back into the room carrying a gun, Temple wondered why his own head began to leak red droplets onto his white paper, and then he thought about it. And as he fell back onto the floor he remembered a word which he thought best described the situation: "Melodrama."

TRIP OF THE TENSES

Sometimes I wonder, wonder if all this is really real.

I think of what I am and what I could be if I wanted to.

Maybe, a musician, an actor, or perhaps a writer. But instead, all I have to look forward to is getting up in morning and going to bed at night.

I look at my friend's face, deep into his eyes, and remember what it was like to live, to feel good. Just to feel is something that is denied.

There is a strong aroma that lives just off the bottom of my nostrils, plays havoc with my nerve endings.

The voice behind me simply said, "Elijah," and I knew he was right.

I turned around and tried to laugh but my teeth and gums just bled. Someone came into the and wiped the remains from my chin and I tried to mumble thanks but several of my molars fell out.

There was some music playing in the foreground, Italian love songs, reminding me of Paris: De-Da-De-Da-De-Da.

So many tenses, continuously switching from Past to Present, that I am sure that this is all too unfamiliar. Very annoying at the best of times.

A smiling face wouldn't go amiss as she comes into the room and taps on my shoulder, whispers into my ear, "Dance for one, you might as well dance for them all." This time I was able to smile which tasted rusty.

The door opened and a hooded shape came into the room. He was surrounded by three fiery imps which swirled around his head. If that was me I would have tried to hit them with a fly swat, but then if it was me they would have hung me with their little heart strings. The hooded figure tries to find somewhere to sit but has to be contented with folding in on himself and falling to the floor in a heap, much to the amusement of the flying munchkins who almost collide with laughter.

The heat is turned up and I feel so cold. The slab beneath me is causing me severe back problems and I can hear my moles and freckles talking to one another while the hair on the back of my legs and abdomen dance in the wind.

Strange, because there is no wind. Only in the mind perhaps. And that has problems of its own!

On of the white walls, opposite the rounded door, there is a painting half-hidden of a boy crying. And at the boy's mouth there are several spiders twisting in their webs, trying to colour his tears in.

The sun goes down and the snow melts and the large oak tree which has been standing for over five thousand years wilts and dies. A man in white comes into the room and sweeps the bundle of clothes into his dustpan and trots out on his hindlegs.

I close my eyes for a split second. In front of me is a warrior of olden times. Half of his armour is missing and he seems to have three legs. He takes off his helmet, revealing a creature indeed: no hair, two black eyes and a long brown face. He spears the flying imps with his lance and roasts them over the camp fire.

"I was looking for Camelot. I know he came this way. But I lost him a few miles down the river. Have you seen him?"

I have to laugh to myself - I cannot do this in person because the things I need for laughing (glands, chemicals, toxins, ghosts) were removed the last time I was here. The little burnt imps have climbed out of his mouth and run away taking the knight's helmet with them. I heard that they had used it as a little house, with a nice green garden and a broken well with a red scorpion at the bottom.

I raise a finger which seems to weigh a ton, and point in several directions. He rides away on a bright red Ladybird.

A voice inside my head shouts, "For my life a secret!"

But I know no secrets. I sold them for my pleasures.

A giant onion spins in front of my eyes and I imagine what it is like not to breath, to be a brain tumour. I ask myself if am stupid and I begin to scratch at my arms because I can feel thousands and thousands of tiny worms burrowing under my skin.

A red and blue snake slithers into the room and gives me some tablets to swallow. It has to force them down my throat because my tongue has gone solid; there's no fluid left in my body.

They begin to work almost instantly, my brain working to full capacity.

So I pull down my shades, give the Tortoise the finger, put the car into first gear and drive away, making strange shadows into the moonlight...

PERSONAL ALIEN

I was sitting outside on the roof, smoking a cigarette when I realised that I was alone. I had family, friends, friends and family, but I was still alone. I also realised that I had been alone for most of my life. I flicked the butt into the night, leant back, and blew the last of the smoke from my lungs and thought. Thought how sad and hard it was. Feelings of melancholy come quick to some people and I'm afraid that I'm one of those.

Lying back on the roof tiles themselves I looked deep into the moon and shouted at it.

"I'M A MAN! I'M HUMAN! I NEED SOMEONE!"

But the moon declined to answer, refused my calls. So I just stared at it a bit longer, swore at the stars and then climbed off the roof and went back into my bedroom via the window and collapsed onto my bed.

It had begun to rain so I closed my entrance to the outside world and pulled the curtains shut.

"There must be something better than all this," I thought. My friends had loves, passions and lust and in my mind they lived. While I who definitely had lust and passions, certainly didn't have loves. I remembered a line from a song that went something like, "Poor is the man whose pleasure depends on the permission of another."

But I didn't agree. I needed, longed for another person to either give me or refuse me permission! Just the opportunity would be enough! The experience essential.

I had had loves though locked in the mistakes of time. But the wind of solitude had blown my way often and I had forgotten what it was like, the feelings, the ecstasy and the broken minds, broken spirits, broken hearts. I needed a new wind, a new force to take me to the boundaries of Heaven and remove me from the gateways of Hell - the Devil's carrion picking at my flesh while God's angels laughed at my plight - mocking my anger, mocking my life.

It was the next day and I was waiting in the bar. I gently and slowly sipped from a bottle of Pils, enjoying the cold liquid coolly and silently slipping down my throat. Everywhere around me there were people, laughing, kissing, angry looking. I was at odds with myself and with them because although I was part of them, I was also their enemy. I noticed at that point in time that I have too many inhibitions about myself to become one, integrate with them to become them, be their equal. Too many nights I had drunkenly and foolishly phoned girls I knew at two in the morning begging for their forgiveness, their love, their oneness with society. But on each of these occasions it was always the same kind of response: "I'm tired Stuart. Can we talk about this in the morning?"

And when the morning came there would be no talk, no speech, no lecture; just a long cold stare.

The usual.

I had ordered another drink, still waiting, when the doors swung open, and while I spied the bottom of my empty bottle I felt a tap on my shoulder and a voice said: "Hello Stuart. I am from the past."

I looked at her, a girl, a woman - early twenties, long reddish hair, white face, nice figure - but if I knew her then, I certainly didn't know her now! I stared deeply into her eyes, read her soul as she flicked back her hair, and as the barman replaced my drink.

"I'm sorry. I don't know you."

She said her name, but it fluttered past my ears. She whispered into my ear, "I'm from the future."

The girl laughed and flung herself around the bar, dislodging drinks, dislodging tables, chairs.

"Come with me, Stuart. Feel the wind! Free the mind. I'm sent from the future to rekindle the past. Re-light youth's angry dream. Be with me, experience love, dream life."

People around me began to stare. First at her and then at me, then at the both of us. I was angry at first but then I was happy. I did want to be with her, be like her. So I joined her dancing around the wreckage, singing to her and to myself.

And everybody joined in. One last Waltz in the Great Room, music rang from our ears, stirred the soul, cracked open the emotions.

But then the barman called time and that was that.

It was like a bad episode from Fame. We all looked at each other and filtered out of the door, for some, never to return.

I lost her in the rush. Someone had let go of the fire alarm. I spent the rest of the afternoon looking for her, but I never saw her again. I went home.

That night I sat on the rooftop. I looked at the moon and raised a glass at it. It was then that I realised that the moon had never left me through the good or through the bad times.

I whispered thanks and went to sleep. I was my own personal alien.

And I liked it.

ELECTION BLUES

It was clear that the election was beginning to get on everybody's nerves. But there were only a few more days to go and it would all be over.

The black transit vans pulled into Eden, Pasadena at about seven in the morning.

The daughter, Annie, was getting ready for school, and as usual the rest of the Routledge family were up. Thomas had already left for work hours ago - and was going to be away for a couple of days, so Melissa had the house to run. But she didn't mind because the death of Donald - only three months old - had really brought the family closer together.

There was a knock at the door and Melissa was brought back to reality. She looked at the large clock on her daughter's wall. It read seven a.m. and she wondered who the hell it was. She sighed and, leaving Annie upstairs to fend for herself, she bolted down the stairs, still with two hairclips hanging from the corner of her mouth.

KNOCK KNOCK-

"Yeah. Hang on a moment! I'm just coming."

KNOCK KNOCK-

"Can't you hear me? I'll be there in a second!"

KNOCK KNOCK-

She reached the latch, saw a blurred shape behind the frosted glass.

KNOCK KNO-

Melissa opened the door.

There was a man wearing a white costume, complete with white spectacles and baseball cap. In his hand he was holding a brilliant white clipboard. Across his chest the words "VOTE FOR CHIP".

"Mommy! Mommy!"

Melissa turned her head and saw her daughter trying to climb over the safety barrier at the top of the stairs. As there was still silence from the intruder she calmly ran up the stairs and grabbed her offspring.

When she returned the front door was securely closed and the stranger was standing next to the hatstand. Smiling. He extended his hand towards Melissa who, very unsurely shook it. She felt confused and annoyed because she didn't recollect closing the door or more importantly inviting him in.   The man chose this moment to start reading from his questionnaire with all the emotion and finesse of a cheap IBM computer.

It must have been the weather or tiredness because Melissa found herself spewing forth answers to questions that normally she wouldn't dare tell a soul - not even her husband, let alone a prospective government official.   She spoke of her private life, her sexual experiments with her sister and the boy next door.   Everything came out and Melissa didn't have a care in the world.   She just talked and looked into his wide blue eyes.

Annie began to cry and the man reached out to comfort - this was the only excuse Melissa had for his action - the wanton child.   But she erupted into a screaming fit.   Melissa glanced up at the clock on the wall...

...three o'clock?

She sees herself in front of the television, laughing at a gameshow, the stupidity of the contestants, when a mixture of blood and adrenaline flows through the body.

She feels a dark soul behind her.

As she senses movement her blood chills (time in slow motion), she turns, she is in a blue-lighted room, gloved hands, cold as ice, close around her neck and - start to squeeze...

...She pulled Annie away from the groping hands.

Again, and for reassurance, she looked up at the clock.

Quarter past seven.

His arm hung in mid-air for what seemed eternity and then he let it fall down by his side.   Melissa could feel the hot red blush of embarrassment rising from her neck to her cheeks, but the man didn't seem to notice.

He stuttered briefly and then resumed asking his questions...

...Melissa daydreams.

She can feel herself falling, falling so very fast, but she doesn't care because she is so tired.

She is lying on something, in something,

something cold,

something oblong...

A COFFIN?!!

Except that it isn't.

It is the bathtub.

She tries to move but she can't, she can't holler for help but she CAN see, yes by God, she can see, the world rejoice, but standing over her is that same man, that same sardonic smile across his face, a long knife in his bony hands.

As he lets it fall, she sees it fall, and expects to feel the pain, but instead,

nothing,

only the sound of dripping

and the clock chimes; five fifteen.

When Melissa opened her eyes Annie was dressed and lying asleep on the sofa. She was sitting in the chair, beneath the windows. The man was still there, sitting at the dining table ticking boxes on his sheet and sipping coffee from one of her mugs.

Her limbs were relieved of their numbness within seconds and she just stared starry-eyed at the man.

He stood up, which for some reason, disturbed her.

"Thank you for participating. Chip would be very pleased if you would vote for him in the election. And on the basis of these answers, Chip is definitely the choice for you. Be comforted to know that all the data given and collected today will be kept in the strictest confidence and will not be sold to any market research company. Again, thank you."

He handed over a bag of goodies. There was a badge, like his own, that seemed to hum with brightness, but it was only a trick of the light.

He walked to the door, leaving Melissa dumbstruck.

And he was gone.

And it was a quarter to eight.

"Come on little girl. Time you went to school."

The whole town was covered by the election volunteers within a few hours.

It was three in the afternoon when the black vehicles pulled away.

The first recorded death that night was that of little Annie. Melissa was trying to put her daughter to bed when Annie suddenly went into fierce convulsions. Melissa grabbed the cause of the pain.

The badge.

She now wished that she hadn't given the gift to her daughter, even though she had whined for ages about it.

The badge had seemed to burn through the fabric of Annie's sweatshirt and was fusing with her skin. The pin itself was growing, digging through the chest. Searching for the entrance to her soul: the heart.

The screaming increased and with it came the blood. Her mother tried to calm her daughter, but there was no way she could remove the badge from the body or stop the eyes from rolling, the body from jumping.

And then, as soon as it had started, it ceased.

Annie convulsed for the final time as her limbs fell rigid. Her eyes fluttered to the top of her head, blood flowed down her legs and at last, with the sound of hissing air, the badge fell from the body, leaving no trace of penetration.

Melissa fell to the floor with a thud, and dreamt of her daughter.

Minutes later two men came into the room. They had come for the body.

"It should have been you," one said. He undid his jacket and the creature fell to the ground.

After they took the first body away, they came for the second. The man put the creature back into his clothes, staining the front red, and left.

The two bodies were deposited in their hearse-like van. And then they started up next-door's pathway. They let themselves in.

All this however, did not go unnoticed.

Gary had known all day that something was wrong. Call it tramp's intuition, he thought, I was bloody right. As he lay hiding in the compost he had seen whole families thrown in the back of those vans.

About three hours later, the black vans pulled away. Tomorrow other people would come, continuing the cycle. HIS work was complete for another decade.

After they had driven away, Gary waited for a couple of minutes and gathering his belongings together - three Safeway carrier bags and a Tesco trolley - he headed fast in the other direction.

As he left the town yards behind him, he met a stray white dog. Several steps further on the faithful hound found something that Gary liked the look of. It was a brand new white coat. He looked at the one he was wearing - smelling and full of holes. He took it off and threw it into the woods.

Wearing his new garment he bent down and made a fuss of the dog who returned his emotions by barking and wagging his tail ferociously and finally licking his new master's face.

"I'm going to call you 'Lucky'."

As it started to rain, Gary buttoned his new coat, but he failed to see the badge.

The badge that glowed...

...later, when the dog stopped barking, a black van pulled away.

TORMENT

Rainsmokeblooddeathscreamssilence

Opening my eyes I imagined I was cold, so cold. I cried openly and cared less when they stained the sand beneath my feet.

But there was no sand, just a small black hole in one of the walls to the side of me and a huge window in front of me which was covered with a thick membrane that seemed to float in an invisible wind. Through this window I could see deep into another room, quite like my own. I looked down at myself and I saw that I was wearing a long white gown and although I was standing I found it difficult to move because I was strapped to the surface behind me via a leather harness.

It was sometime later. The heat had been turned up to some ungodly level and I was sweating profusely. The black hole had grown somewhat larger while I stared with abundance into the window. There, the room was not empty like my own. There were about five people all wearing gowns such as mine except that they were green in colour. Dark, dark green with little masks and hats that covered the most of their ugly features. One by one they would come to my window and mumble something - although I couldn't understand completely what they were saying, they seemed to be very sad. In fact, one woman in particular seemed to be very emotional and I could see clearly two tear stains on her cheeks. For a moment or two I was sure that I recognised the odd face or two but when all you could see was an eye here and a nose there it would be hard to recognise your own mother.

I think it was the morning but I can't be sure. I don't even remember being asleep but my arm was hurting as if a needle had pricked it. There was a small red dot on my limb and a trail of the red substance leading to the black hole which now covered half of the wall. But as my arm was hanging loosely I was pleased, if only for a moment. I was sure that I could hear music, however it was dull like as if it was being played from the bottom of a well. I can not be positive but I was sure that it was one of my favourite pieces of music, 'The Blue Danube' by Strauss. Memories played havoc with my mind. So I closed my eyes and thought for a while.

There was a voice that seemed to bounce off all the walls in my white room which would then vanish down the black hole. I think that it was the voice of my mother and when I decided to open my eyes there were two people looking at me through the window. I tried to shout at them but the noise I made only hurt my ears. Both my arms were free and while one scratched the stubble on my chin the other tried to set me free. However the strap was behind the small of my back and neither of my hands could reach it. I was starting to worry because all the time the black hole was moving decidedly closer to my harness.

I stared in horror as the two people shook their heads. My stubble had now become a long white beard down to my ankles, which I could not see properly because half of my lower legs had vanished down the black hole. The view from my window had now changed and I saw some kind of monitor with a straight light green line that was non-moving. I tried to scream but all I felt was severe pain as if I was being electrocuted. All my body hair had been shaved away and instead of leaning against the wall I was now lying on the floor. As I lay there wilting and withering occasionally I would catapult into the air which left deep red marks upon my chest.

I stared out of the window, it was all I could do. The black hole mocked me and promised to swallow me whole. I was ready to give up the ghost when I saw the people hurry around the monitor. The straight line began to move and a little green light appeared, which although it did nothing at first soon begun to jump about. It reminded me of one of those old computer games from the 70's. My view soon turned to the people who started to embrace each other. It was then that I realised that I could actually hear the noise that the monitor made and while I smiled the black hole seemed to scream as it melted back the way it had come and ultimately disappeared. I mocked it back.

I was able to stand up and the window opened and beckoned me.

As I climbed through it a voice shouted, "AWAKEN!"

And I returned the comment, "Resurgam."

The white room and the glass window shattered.

It was much, much later. I opened my eyes.

I hoarsely whispered, "Where am I?"

"Don't worry about that at the moment Mr. Garner. You've been in a coma for the last five years. We thought we had lost you but eh... something happened. I suppose you could call it a miracle."

THE SOUL-LIFTER

The Voices. They were evil tonight. Once the carnage began they fell silent.

Hunger. Blood. Power. He felt exalted. He was a God. He was a monster. Admiring his handiwork he used his elongated fingers to smear the offal all over his haunched body. And flung the carcass across the room.

After the pressure: relief. At last. A weekend away. The past weeks had been hell but now she had the chance to drive to the country. See Becky. Forget it, my job is over. Got to get away. What the hell, I haven't seen Becky for a couple of weeks now. Strange, I haven't even had a letter or phone-call. But her work as an illustrator was even more arduous than that of a publisher. But then, thinking of the thatched roof, the tiny rooms, the open fire, heaven. On earth. She threw her bags in the back of her battered Beetle, indicated right and drove away.

Blessed. Special. The Chosen One. This is how his Deity called to him. It could be at any time. He was glad of the company. Oh! How those other Voices tired him! Made him weak! No! He must be strong! There was work to be done. The words of Milton were burnt into his skin:

I GIVE NOT HEAVEN FOR LOST. FROM THIS DESCENT CELESTIAL VIRTUES RISING, WILL APPEAR MORE GLORIOUS AND MORE DREAD THAN FROM NO FALL, AND TRUST THEMSELVES TO FEAR NO SECOND FATE.

With his talons he scratched at the words, felt the meaning leak from his body. He suckled upon his feast and began to weep. Not tears of sadness but of jubilation.

The Voice had been with him since the Awakening. This was on his sixteenth birthday. While his hand enjoyed, his mind lay dormant and the Voice called to him. Just his name. Simplicity. But as the days passed, the Voice became stronger and stronger and while he played less with his friends and more with himself, the Voice told

Jonathan about his Purpose here on earth. The Grand Plan. The end of man in his present form.

Jonathan was instructed to kill his father. It wasn't as hard as he thought it would be. Looking back at it now he seemed such a sissy. A coward. But then of course he had had to use conventional weapons. He hadn't been graced with the tools he had now.

His mother had died in childbirth. His father blamed him. Every single minute of every single hour of every single day he was reminded of the fact. His father did nothing but sit at home, drink, and watch a porn film. And, remind his boy that he was responsible for the death of his wife. Not that Jonathan was without a mother but that he was devoid of a woman. A hole for his cock. Base terms. Base facts.

The authorities had found Jonathan in the kitchen, in a cupboard, chewing on one of his father's leg bones. There was blood all over the house. Most of course on the bedroom wall, along with his father's head, genitals stuffed in his mouth.

And still the Voice demanded more. However this Voice had been joined by another. That of his father. Who begged for his son's forgiveness. It was the drink talking!

"Son, I love you. YOU ARE ALL I HAVE LEFT!" And begged to be released. This, it seemed, was part of the deal. You capture the Voice, the soul of the victim and store it inside you, feel its pain, live its pleasure.

A lot of water had flowed under the bridge since then, however. Here he was, twenty years later, finally out of prison, released on his own merit. If only they knew! The nights in the remand centre that the Voice helped him transform and escape. The days in prison when he feigned illness and went OUTSIDE.

So now, quite a conversation was building up inside his head. He imagined his mind as a large black room. His Master was on one side, on the other his captives. He was somewhere in the middle. Caught in the crossfire. Hating every minute.

The sun was on the decline. Sheryl hoped that Becky was in because she wasn't in the mood for hanging around. She wanted to get inside, collapse in front of the fire and open the nearest bottle of Vodka. In their Uni days Becky and she had made quite a name for themselves around campus for their vast intakes of drink. Nothing had changed in the passing years, except for the furrows and crow lines on both of their faces.

When she pulled into the driveway she noticed several changes. The garden seemed a little more wild and even the roof, which was Becky's pride and joy was out of control. There were patches here and there that needed immediate attention. Once out of the car Sheryl tried her best to look through the back window but both curtains were closed tightly shut. She went back round to the front and tried the main door. It was locked. She knocked several times. Nothing. She knocked again. Nothing. Sheryl remembered that Becky kept a spare key somewhere in the back garden. But she wasn't dressed for an expedition into the undergrowth.

The best thing to do was to go down the road to the local pub. They had a telephone and there was also a good chance that Becky was there, having a drink. Sheryl got back into the car, opened her purse, took out pencil and paper, jotted down a message and posted it through the letterbox. Within seconds she was back in the car and driving away.

Jonathan had a splitting headache. The Voices were giving him a nightmare time. One minute they shouted. The next they whispered. He wasn't sure which was worse. With his Master's help he had been able to keep control, but he knew the time was just round the corner when they would be victorious. Snuff out his own life. Death from the inside. An implosion of cells.

He readily prepared himself! He went into the bathroom and turned on the shower. As the water ran down his body, washing away previous stains, he wished he could wash away the Voices. He was becoming more and more confused because everyday was becoming progressively harder to live. He was even finding it more difficult to transform, which angered the Master, who was able to pierce his mind like a lance.

"Have you got any change for the 'phone?"
"Sure, what do you want?"
"Tens, twenties. I've got a pound."
"Here you are."
"Thanks. I'll have a vodka and orange, please. There's some money there. Take what you need."

She tried Becky's number several times but there was no answer.

"No luck then?"

"Er... no. It's been one of those days."

"Oh yeah?"

"I've come up from the big smoke to see my friend. You might know her. Rebecca Marlton? We've both been in here a few times. Although I don't remember your face."

"Rebecca Marlton? Aye. She's that painter isn't she? She's been here a few times, but not for a couple of months. June, I think it was. I only took this pub in May. Yeah. June it was."

"June? My God I didn't believe it had been so long! I've been so busy with one thing or the other. I can't believe it!"

There was a pause. The landlord walked up to the other end of the bar. While Sheryl sipped at her drink, he returned with a photograph.

"Here she is, look. I had this done the day I moved in. The bar was heaving."

Sheryl studied the picture more closely. It was definitely Becky. But who was that man she seemed to be talking to? It could have been anyone.

"Ask around the bar if you want. She's probably at home working. You know what these kind of people are like. Work unsociable hours. Sleep during the day. Come out at night."

"I know how she feels."

"Oh. Are you a painter as well?"

"Becky is an illustrator. No, I work in the publishing business. Same kind of hours."

"Illustrator? Ah, I see. Like I said, you are welcome to talk to anyone. And if you need somewhere to stay tonight then we have a spare room. Reasonable rates."

"Okay. Thanks. I don't recognise many of the faces. But I'll have a go anyway. And you better make that bed up. I think I'll be needing it."

"Same again?"

Her glass was empty.

"Yeah, why not? I might as well enjoy myself."

The landlord returned with another.

"Here you are. On the house. The name's Beckett. Samuel Beckett."

"Sheryl Cox. And thanks."

"That's alright. Anything for a young lady."

He winked, and walked away.

"Okay, here goes," Sheryl thought and wandered off into the milling crowd.

Jonathan admired himself in the mirror.

The Voice told him that one more was all he needed. The future hung in the balance. Even the Voices were quiet. Maybe, after all their shouting, they had resigned themselves to the fact that the Master was close to his transformation here on earth. But Jonathan doubted it. After having a lie down for a little while at nine o'clock, Jonathan left his flat.

Sheryl was sitting at one of the smaller tables. She had talked to a few people but although they professed their love and affection for the local celebrity, they too admitted that they hadn't seen her for sometime. There were various explanations for this: she was out of town, she had run away, she was a vampire, she was married, she had stopped drinking. None of these seemed plausible. But there was one other notion. Maybe she had had an accident and had died in agony calling out for her friends? Sheryl felt all hot and flustered. Maybe Becky WAS dead. No! No, don't be stupid. She's not dead! It's just the drink talking. And reading too many Clive Barker novels!

She moved as the man she was talking to stumbled off to the toilet. She found herself propping up the bar. There was some kind of disco going on in the other bar, music thumping, strobe light flashing. But before the next song came on she heard the main door bang open and shut. After downing another drink she turned around.

"Now there's a man with problems," she thought. Standing and frowning. Scratching his head as if trying to rub something away. Bad memories probably. He was about thirty-five. Smart. Dark hair. Brown eyes, tanned complexion. Six two, twelve or thirteen stone. Probably a banker. Or a spy. Now where do I know him from? Oh yes! It was the man in the photo with Becky. God, he didn't look that tall when he was sitting down. Yeah, he might know something about the disappearance. It's a long shot. He walked over to the bar.

"Hey mister!"

Nothing.

"Hey you! Tall guy! Want a drink?"

Recognition.

"Yeah. Come over here. Sit down."

"Hello," strained.

"Hello to you too. D'ya want a drink or what? You look like shit. What's the matter, girlfriend trouble?"

"No. Just a splitting headache. It's been with me over the years. We're old companions."

"Right. So why the gloves?"

"The what?"

"THE GLOVES. Why are you wearing the gloves?"

"Oh. Force of habit really. Wear them for this and that, you know."

"You don't look the type."

"The type?"

"You know. Labourer. Engineer. Whatever."

Beckett returns.

"What will you be having?"

"Two vodkas. Fine yeah?"

The man nodded.

"Yeah. Two vodkas please."

The drinks flow. The conversation stutters. She asks about Becky and the photo. He orders more drinks. She asks again. He says he knows nothing about it. A casual conversation. More drinks. She thinks he's lying. He's quiet for a little while. Asks her about herself, her name, her age, where she lives. More drinks. She forgets about Becky.

"I'll be back in a sec, I need the toilet."

Thumping music. Strobe lights. Toilet outside. Long trek. She goes. She feels something beside her. In front of her. In her. A creature. A man. A monster. Claws. Mouth. A snarl. A feeling. Ready to pounce. She cowers against the wall. The toilet door. He stops. Something in his mind. A cry! "The Voices." Ramshackle, rumpus. The creature's mind. Begins to scratch at himself. Grabs the girl. Screams. Howls. Piercing. Music. Light. She tears, she pulls. Again: "the Voice!" Then: "No." The music stops. The lights come on. She takes a long time to walk back. Slowly. Carefully. She leaves the body.

The bloodied woman returned, fell into the arms of the landlord.
It's over. It's over.

Later, when it was all quiet and the police had gone, in her mind she heard, "Hi Sheryl. It's Becky. Long time no see."

SHE DREAMS OF ALBERT

She hadn't always been a lesbian, and she wasn't quite sure if she was a complete lesbian, maybe three-quarters, maybe half. Tonight however, her dreams were with Albert. Albert Constantine. She had met him on holiday in America, and despite what her other friends said about men (ie, they made their blood curdle), Albert was different. She was excited by him.

As usual, it was at a party. She had dressed pretty well stereotypically: short hair, jeans, baggy tee-shirt - trying to hide the fact that she was a woman. She didn't really mind wearing men's clothes, as most of her friends did, but now and again, she revelled in wearing a dress, and make-up. Because she liked someone of the same sex, she didn't understand why society tried to make her wear something she didn't feel comfortable with.

She had been standing by the bar with the closest friend she had at college who had gone with her on this 'holiday', a trip to the Shrine-the "Gay capital of the world", San Francisco - Babra. They had been there for some time, but today Babra was coming on a bit strong. She was five years older and far more experienced, so much so that she went for what she wanted straight away, ignoring the protests and whims of her prospective partner.

She turned her head away as Babra tried to kiss her neck and her eyes fell on a boy, who looked so unhappy, just standing in the doorway with a solitary tulip in his hand. Babra grabbed her non-drinking hand, which was the final straw.

"I'm going to party. I'll talk to you in a bit."

"Whatever."

She walked over to the boy. On closer study he was quite handsome, about twenty, but he looked far younger. She wondered if he had started shaving yet. She would have loved to have shown him the 'first time', careful not to spill any of his precious fluid.

"Yes."

"Pardon."

"Yes I am on my own."

"Oh right! Sorry! I was miles away."

"The name is Albert. Albert Constantine. I love your accent. Is it Australian?"

"Er... no. English."

"You're from London, right? I've heard so much about London. The Queen, Big Ben, The Tower. Great eh? Anyway, what is all that shit with Charles and Di, anyway?"

"I'm not sure. And no. I'm not from London. Cornwall. It's quite a distance."

He fell quiet.

"So... Hi Albert. My name is Alexandra Carter. But most of my friends just call me Alex."

"Pleased to meet you."

They shook hands.

"Wait there a minute Alex. I'll just get myself a drink."

"Okay."

As Albert walked away, she looked around for Babra. Not that she cared anymore. She wanted just to see that she was alright, and was not getting herself into any trouble.

Babra was okay. She was chatting up some blonde bimbo on the stairs.

"No competition," Alex thought. "But hey! Let her have a good time!"

She felt a tap on her shoulder. She turned. Albert was back.

"Okay, Alex?"

"Yeah. Fine. Thanks."

"I had a little trouble getting a drink. Some dyke tried to chat me up."

"Oh. Right."

She then added, "Kiss me Albert. Kiss me."

So he did.

A little later they were sitting out in the backyard, watching the moonlight, the stars, and hearing the sounds of the night creatures, occasionally broken by the noise of someone vomiting.

"I have got something here you might like to see," Alex murmured.

"Oh, what is it?"

Albert shot up, immediately excited.

"THIS, YOU BASTARD!"

She pulled out a knife and slit his neck, and danced as his fiery blood covered her body. She had no choice but to drink wholeheartedly.

"Ready to leave yet?"

Babra had walked out into the death of the boy.

"Yes."

"Are you okay?"

"Do you know something?"

"No. What?"

"I hate being called a dyke!"

They kissed passionately as they flew into the night and both dreamed of Albert.

SOUL SOLDIER

A feeling. Nothing more.

A feeling of dread, of hunger and thirst.

There were many voices, both inside and out, but there was one he could hear clearly, one that replayed over and over in his head. And that voice spoke just one word: "Dead."

That night it was so very cold in the seventeenth century mortuary, which three hundred years later was still in full working use.

"I suppose that's progress," thought Joey Devlin, the resident mortician. Those people who didn't know him might wonder what he was doing in a place like this, but he had his reasons. If anyone ever had to look for Joey (and I'm not saying that anyone did) you would usually find him in the graveyard, speaking aloud the inscriptions like some ancient gothic chant.

Joey never spoke to many people (not live ones anyway!), and not many spoke to Joe either. So it was somewhat of a surprise when he thought he had heard his name being called. He was sitting at his desk reading the latest horror novel by the light of a newly waxed candle when one of the drawers in the large cabinet behind him slid open. He had heard the noise straight away because they hadn't been oiled in such a long time.

He put the book down onto the table and moved the glow of the candle over to the cabinet where the bodies were kept. The light now made strange flickering shadows on the wall, like dancing elves. It was true, one of the drawers had in fact come open!

Joey listened again, but there was no repeat calling. The label on the drawer gave certain details about the inhabitant but he wasn't interested. He pushed at the drawer and, although at first it was quite stubborn, it eventually gave way. Joey fixed the lock and returned to his book.

Several pages had been read when he thought he heard the voice again. He turned around and refocused the light on the cabinet.

"Hey, turn that light away man! It's hurting my eyes!"

Joey froze.

"Come on man! I can't see."

The flame from the candle revealed a black man of about twenty, sitting up in one of the drawers, hands covering his eyes.

Joey moved the light away, but was still too shocked to speak.

"Wow! Thanks. I thought I was going to be blind. You can't have a blind dead man, can you? What's the matter with you? The devil got your tongue? The man let out a raspy laugh.

"It's been a long time since I done of those."

He laughed again. Then he coughed up some blue-green blood, which he wiped away with the white sheet that was covering him.

"Sounds like you've got a bad cough there sir. Would you like a little water? I haven't got anything stronger."

"There's a bottle of Bourbon in the pipe behind the wastepaper basket. Carter keeps it in there. Thinks that no-one knows about it, but we all do!"

"Oh! l didn't know."

The man the body was referring to was Carter Madison, who worked during the day. Carter was almost the only one who said anything to Joey, but then it was only "hello" or "good-bye."

Joey put his hand behind the basket into the pipe and felt around.

"It's in there somewhere, man."

"Got it. You were right mister!"

"Hey, enough of the 'mister'. Didn't you read my tag? Look I've got another hanging around my toe. The name's Alexander Henry. Come over here. Shake my hand. I'm nothing to be scared of. Us dead'uns have had some bad press but that's why I'm here."

Joey walked slowly over to the man, who was now leaning against the cabinet.

"I'd better pull this here blanket up. I don't want you seeing all my particulars or a hole as big as a football where my chest should be. That steel rod just went right through me. Oh well not to worry, I hated that job. And if I wasn't dead then I wouldn't have had the chance to meet you."

"I suppose not Mr. Henry. Here's your Bourbon."

"Thanks. Just call me Alex. Okay?"

"All right."

Alex took a couple of swigs of the drink, let out a gasp and gave the bottle back to Joey.

"Go on, try a little."

"Er... no, it's okay."

"Hey, it won't kill you. Look I'm still ali... Well, you know what I mean."

"Okay, just a sip."

Joey looked at the bottle and then put it to his mouth, waiting a couple of seconds, took a sip and then swallowed.

"Orrgghh!" he squealed, demonstrating a face like a squashed pig.

"Wow, man! You're so funny. How old are you?"

"Twenty-three."

"Twenty-three! And you've never tasted liquor? You are a strange chap. Anyway, what the hell are you doing working in a place like this? You should be out there, enjoying yourself. Get yourself a girl, that's what my old mam used to say. It never failed me."

"I haven't got any friends. Or any family, that's why I'm here."

"No family? Man, what happened?"

Joey waited, went over to the table and sat down in the chair.

"We were heading over Utah way, to see my Grandma. It was my fifth birthday. All I remember is that standing in the middle of the road was the most prettiest woman I have ever seen. My dad swerved to miss her, and the car hit a bank and we tipped over and then all goes black. The next thing I know I'm in the hospital. Everyone was killed except for me."

('Dead.')

The young man fell silent, trying his hardest to force back the tears.

"I went to live in this home and three years ago I got out, and have been living here ever since. I know it sounds strange but since then I've felt that it's been my duty to look after the dead. The living shun me so why can't I live with the dead? Uh?"

Joey put his head into his hands and rested them on the table.

"Hey man! It's okay. Let it all out. It's all right to cry."

Alex rested a hand on Joey's shoulder. Joey jumped at the cold feeling that ran down his spine but didn't move the hand away. Alex handed him the bottle and Joey took a mouthful.

"See it's not that bad, is it?"

"I guess not. Thanks."

"Thanks for what?"

"For this, you know. I've never been able to speak about it. Not to anyone. Can I tell you something else?"

"Yeah, sure. Fire away."

"When I was in hospital I had this dream. I was standing in a large blue room. There was a bed in the centre and Jesus was lying on that bed, asleep. I walked over to him and stared him right in the face. His eyes opened and red tears fell down his cheeks. I turned around and there in the corner of the room was a blinding light. I fell to my knees and a voice ran out around me saying, "He is here."

"I closed my eyes and faced the light and demanded that if He was God then He should return my family. But you know. He didn't."

There was a pause and Alex said, "What's done is done, I suppose. Look, it's almost morning. I can't spend the rest of the night talking. I've got an early start. They're burying me at ten."

"Will I ever see you again?"

"I doubt it. But you never know. When you're dead, ask for Alexander Henry at the gates and we might just get reintroduced."

Alex went back to his drawer, climbed back inside and put the blanket over his body.

"And hey! If you ever see that light again, look into it, man. Look deep into it. As deep as you can imagine. Remember."

He dreamt that night. The same dream that had haunted him since that fateful day. Everything was the same: the bed, Christ on the bed, looking at Christ and then in the background the light. Once again Joey fell to his knees but while the voice was speaking Joey stood up, gathered together all his courage and stared right into his nemesis. The light became heavy but instead of fearing the light, Joey welcomed it and begged its forgiveness.

And as the light welcomed, Joey begged his forgiveness, he heard Christ speak.

He said, "Memphis reconciled."

A force slowly pushed Joey towards the light and he was sure he could make out faces in the distance. A voice from within the light spoke:

"They're all here Joey. Just waiting. Come and touch them man. Reach and touch them."

Joey understood and smiled. He walked deeper into the light, meeting the outstretched hands and clasping them.

Death became life once more.

INSANITY: WRITER'S BLOCK

My name is Daniel Beames and I have come to the assumption that nothing exists beyond the Void. Our imagination can only reach so far, no matter what anyone says. For the first time in years, I'm scared. Scared of the future, scared of the past.

The snow falls past my window. I stare into the whiteness, which in itself is another kind of Void, but not the one I spoke of earlier. There's no doubting that one, that's for sure.

You see, I buried my children yesterday. They died in an automobile accident. They were coming to see me, their widowed father, when a truck jack knifed on the highway. Their car drove straight into it and well... the rest is history. A huge spiral of smoke could be seen from the front porch of old Ma Walker's house. And she lived miles away.

She is a sad old lady. Her boy's got some kind of brain disease, he's a bit slow. Which means he's the laughing stock of the neighbourhood. But he's got a job in the library helping Miss McShelton.

Good for him, bad for her. She hasn't had a good life either. First her mother died and then she got into some scandal with the principal of the local highschool. It's some kind of town I live in isn't it? But I suppose that's life. No question this time. A statement, for sure.

Before, my work always lacked a certain passion, but ever since the death of my wife, novel followed novel and soon I was able to move into this lush apartment in the heart of the city. But I suppose that it's a bit big for me now. As I'm alone.

Alone for now, anyway. Alone with writer's block.

I think I'd better come clean. I'm a sinner. My readers would love this one!

I'm a killer! A cold blooded murderer. Good eh?

Yeah, that's right. It all started the day after my wife died. I was walking aimlessly around the park, drunk as a skunk, a bottle of Southern Comfort in my hand, my clothes hanging like rags and reeking of a distillery, tears running down my already stained cheeks. But something else became stained that day - my soul.

I was carrying one of those black handled knives in my pocket. It had been a present on my wedding day. Our day. The best day in the world. But I wanted to get that bastard and give him a taste of his own medicine.

My wife had been killed in the mall downtown. She was comparing the prices of two dresses when this Chinese guy comes up to her and tries to grab her purse. Being a good citizen, she wouldn't let it go and hung on as hard as she could. He pulled out a gun and shot her twice in the head. As she fell to the ground he ran away.

Until I found him.

I just couldn't let him get away with it.

There were three of them standing in the middle of the park next to a lighted dustbin. The Chinese guy was either stoned or ratted, it made no matter. He was telling the others this story of how he killed this Plutonian disguised as a Martian in the mall. They all started laughing like wolves, but fell silent when I got near them.

I offered them a drink from my bottle, and realizing that I was one of their own they started talking again. The Chinese guy pulled out his revolver and showed it to the others. He now proclaimed that he was working for the Emperor Zarb. I listened and waited.

We waited until it was time to sleep.

Tonight his mind would welcome a new kind of nightmare.

I didn't have that long to wait. A couple of hours, not even that. The others slept huddled together by the dying embers of the fire, sharing each other's heat. Our friend however declared that he was to receive new orders from his masters and it was better that he slept alone. I decided that I would sleep in the playground. There I felt alone, along with the young. There, I felt some kind of comfort. I longed to be a child again. Soaring into the air on the swings, falling off the end of the slide, grazing my knees.

Anyway, I could see better from here.

If I was still drunk (and that I seriously doubt!), I sobered up rapidly. I soon got to work. Out of my pocket I pulled the knife, its blade glistening in the twilight. I stumbled over to where he lay, praying that he was asleep.

My prayer was answered (the first this week!). My life had fallen apart and now I was praying that a wino was dead to the world. Some prayer!

Some God.

Anger.

A river of luck was flowing my way. He had his mouth open so I counted to three and rammed the end of my bottle down his throat. As he started to cough and splutter his eyes opened, tears started to form, matching my own. His limbs started to kick out but before he could get any real motion going I slammed the blade into his belly.

And stabbed...

and stabbed...

and stabbed...

and stab...

I stopped.

I had hit the right spot. His eyes began to roll but I didn't want him to die just yet. The game was not over yet! I knew that I had to be quick. He would soon welcome death.

I pulled the knife from his stomach and removed the bottle from his mouth as he fought for his breath, fighting for release. I stripped him, twice, first, his blood stained clothes, and then his blood stained skin-like splitting celery. I'm not even sure when he died! I lost all sense. All I left was the skin around the genital area. (I wasn't a pervert.)

As the day returned I noticed that I was alone. The others had run, not wanting to stay around while I was at work. I dumped the wastage in an old bin and after collecting some kindling wood I got the fire going again. I walked away.

Of course now I know the huge risk I was taking! What if someone saw me? What if the others spoke?

But nothing did happen, no-one saw me and no-one said anything.

I was free!

When I got home I started to write. And write. And write. The words flowed from my pen only interrupted when, reluctantly, I had to go to my wife's funeral. The children would never have forgiven me. I wore a red rose with my black suit. A memory long since dead.

My book was finished within a week, and once published stayed at the top of the Bestseller's list for over a year. If ever I had writer's block again I would go to the park or the station and get to work. No-one suspected, and I was cured.

My reputation precedes me.
Oh well, I'd better stop now, because I'm just off out.
I've got a job to do for the Intergalactic Space Command.
Each to his own, eh?
My new typewriter's ready.
I think I'm going to be busy for the next couple of days.

JAYNE'S AMERICA

Sitting by the window I shouted at the gloomy surroundings. There was a little Djinn that lived in a bottle and looked back at my world, and, like myself, wondered what life was all about. Endless tremors, tumours, trains like ants flowed through my brain, lighting every sinew, exciting every nerve ending. Bored, I removed the ceremonial knife from its scabbard and slit both my wrists. While I lay in a pool of blood, my underling bolted from its bottle, skipped merrily over and lapped at my soul, laughing at my handicap.

Joe knew it was all over when the "fatman" came through the window. So he dived down behind his desk, pulled out the hidden gun, and tried to survive the scene. Unfortunately for him, he was too late. The fatman fired both barrels of his shotgun instantaneously and laughed loudly to the outside spectators as Joe catapulted against the far wall. As he slid slowly to the floor, leaving red trails of blood and gore on the white paper behind him, Joe thought he was on some mind-bending drug because he had this strange sensation that he was flying through a dark tunnel. And at the end of this tunnel, which he had reached at amazing speed, a small black elephant came into view, held up his trunk and whispered, "Not my graveyard."

There were streets and there were streets. Some good and some bad and some that ranked somewhere in between. What labels a street one thing or another no-one is quite certain, but you definitely knew when you came across a bad street you learnt that it was a good idea to get the hell out as soon as you could. It was on one of these streets that Gary now found himself. He had only been in town a couple of nights, a little naïve, and somehow tonight he had stepped into the wrong neighbourhood. He knew that he had hit trouble as soon as he had made a left at Madison and then a right on Union. People's skin colour changed - although this is not always the reason why a street becomes labelled good or bad - and their souls became darker. All around him Gary could see death and decay. On every street corner he could see pimps and hookers, hookers and pimps.

The same scene everywhere...

A car pulls up to the kerb...

A window let down and the customary, "Looking for a good time mister?"

"How much?"

"Thirty dollars, basic."

"Okay, get in."

Gary moved on, knowing that every step would take him further and further into this underground kingdom, commonly known to the natives as HELL'S KITCHEN. All of the stuff that went on down here was bad news. Bad news on bad streets. A good person such as Gary because he was good, was bound to have trouble knocking at his door. So he walked hurriedly past the tramps, the twilight creatures.

But trouble came looking.

And found Gary.

"Hey buddy!"

"Keep walking, don't say a word."

"I said hey buddy!!"

Ignore it, he's way behind, you keep going.

A touch on his shoulder. He turns around.

"Yeah? Can I help you?"

Three men, quite large, definitely able to handle themselves.

"Give us your money!"

"Ehh?"

They threw him against the wall with a slap and began to pummel his stomach and face. No-one offered to help him. They kicked him in the ribs, took his wallet, his watch. His watch!

And one of them took out a knife. And stripped him of his skin.

We had all come from different routes, but the destination was the same. There were three of us sitting together in a dark, dark room. But there was something comforting about it all the same, despite the darkness.

Accompanying us was one of the Others. It didn't say anything or had said anything all the time we had been in the room. It just sat there and watched as if in judgement but also as if in mockery. As if it was our fault that it was there, as if we were keeping it from some higher accolade.

We looked at each other. There was a tint of sadness in people's faces and also embarrassment. The word, "SPEAK," slipped from the Other's lips and each in turn told our tales.

When we had finished, I remembered perfectly an entry I had written in my diary:

December 13th 1992

"Tonight I have seen a sickness. A sickness so vile, so deprived, so contrived that I know no cure. And if a cure existed, I pity the man that tried to use it."

AMERICA! AMERICA! Blasts from the jukebox.

But no-one is listening, whether it is the words or the implications that have no meaning it makes no difference to me or to them.

"God is to blame," cries a voice.

"Pardon?"

"Inquiries. Transactions. All implications. All defiant."

"Your mind twists from one sector to another. I just can't keep pace with you."

"Think of a beetle," she said. "The way it walks, the way it talks. That's the answer to everything. Want another?"

She took it for granted and ordered, chatting to the barman. The music was turned up and several cheers came from the corner. A woman bumped into me on her way to the toilets. She murmured sorry but took no real notice of me.

A drink was pushed in front of my face so I finished the one in my hand and chuckled to myself.

"Are you okay?" she asked.

"Yeah. Of course."

"What's the matter then? Why are you laughing?"

"All this, my friend, is an illusion. This drink here, is the reality."

"You are so right," she agreed.

So we drank the reality away. We left late and on the way home we hitched a ride in the back of someone's truck. We waved good-bye and fell asleep in a ditch.

The command "LEAVE" brought me back to my senses. And while we filed out of that room to God knows where, I pretended to tip my hat to the Other. And I swear that I saw a smile upon its white lips...

The door hissed behind us.

CONTROVERSIAL SENTINEL

I was wanting a second chance.

So, I waited in a motel room for her. The door was left open and for a little while I stood on the balcony watching the cars drive by. The sun had almost turned the sky red when the lilac Buick drove into the parking lot. I just stood there and stared as she grabbed her bags from the rear seats, got out of the vehicle, and slammed the door behind her. There was an electronic beep as she played with the key. Immediately I went inside and looked at my reflection in the mirror. When I was sure that I was immaculate I returned to the outside. But she was already there, standing in the doorway, blocking the little sunlight that there was. She dropped her bags, ran her fingers through her dark hair. I stopped.

"Mark," she said.

"So you came then," I replied.

"Did you doubt I would?"

"At times."

She hesitated. "Can I come in?"

"Do you want to?"

"Of course."

"Well, come in then"

As she entered, she shut the door behind her.

As she entered, I ran my hands over her body.

I whispered into her ear, "I'm glad you came."

I felt her smile and she said, "So am I."

I soon woke from my dark dreams. The sun had long gone and I decided to venture outside. It was raining. Pouring down. I had never seen the weather so violent, so hungry for blood. I switched on my Walkman, listened to nothing in particular and looked into the night. After a while I began to look at the rain, stare right into its heart. I heard sounds. I switched off my stereo. She was moaning.

"Are you alright?" I asked.

"Yeah," the sleepy reply.

"Go back to your nightmares."

I looked deeper into the rain and I swore that I could see a face in the bushes by the roadside.

I felt tired and went back inside.

"To hell with the truth!" I thought.

Sleep came quickly.

Light filtered through my eyelids, so I thought it must have been morning. There was someone sitting at the end of my bed.

"I am the Sentinel," he said.

I reached but she was no longer there.

"She is dead," the stranger whispered.

In my hand. An axe. Blood dripping on the floor, staining the carpet. I must have killed her recently. The pain in my head hurt. Her pain was so, so, sweet. I laughed. And he laughed.

There was some writing, in bold, red letters, on her white pillow. It read, "SO YOU ARE LEFT FOR DEAD." Written with a finger.

I didn't understand what it meant exactly so I turned the pillow over, knocking the axe to the floor and spilling a bowl of blood which I was keeping for later, as I did so.

I looked at the stranger. He was now hooded, his face hidden. He was different from the ones I had seen in my dreams. He moved to the couch, sat down, while I lay in the wet patch and longed to be king.

I lit up a cigarette, "So what do you want?"

"You, of course," the stranger muttered.

"Shall we dance then?" I asked, scooping the brains from her skull and stubbing the cigarette out on my arm.

When I looked up he had gone.

For five nights I sat by my bed. The blood had long since dried on the walls and I thought it looked quite decorative along with the pictures of flowers and the fake Dalis. My bags were packed and waiting by the door. I hadn't washed, changed my clothes or really eaten since he had last been here. It was as if I didn't want to miss my chance. A chance at what I wasn't really too sure.

I picked at my teeth with a splinter of one of her rotting bones and suddenly felt a hot flush of air. My tool fell to the floor as I stood up. I was nervous as hell, but there was a sense of calm. There were two this time and I thought that this was better.

"Shall we go then?" I asked.

"Of course."

I picked up my bags.

"Oh no. Where we are going, you will not need them."

"Okay," I said, and dropped them.

I grabbed their hands, and followed them through the wall.

Ever since I was a small child I have always wanted to walk through walls, but as I took the first step I knew that I had made a serious mistake. My left foot felt like jelly and my hands were slippery. There was no support from my legs, my spine was ready to give way. When. There was a blinding white light.

My eyes soon recovered. I was lying on a huge stone in some kind of tomb. There was an ethereal being at my head and at my feet. There was some writing on one of the walls. It was in Latin:

"TERRIBILIS EST LOCUS ESTE". I sat up.

There was a scraping sound and an entrance appeared in front of me. A woman came into the tomb. As she did so the beings motioned for me to stand up. As I did so, the woman fell to the floor, by my feet and whispered, "Lord."

A second chance...

A GRAND FINALE

The truth had come out. It was a grand disaster!

He put away into the drawer, his needle, the small packet of white powder and his other equipment. He settled back. A chaffinch flew into the room and sat on the desk, slowly pecking at his text. A harsh wind blew, sending his life's work throughout the room. All he could do was watch as several pieces of paper fluttered silently out of the window.

Later, when it was sunny, she came into the room. A sense of serene normality had returned (if only partial), and when she asked if he was alright, he was able to reply "fine".

"How is it going?" she wondered, sitting beside him on the couch.

He collected what was left of his manuscript together into a messy pile. The bird had knocked over a pot of ink and now all over the desk there were small blue clawprints.

"Yeah, alright I think."

"Any idea when it will be finished?"

She examined her nails.

"Soon. I hope so anyway. It's already four months overdue and we ran out of money weeks ago."

"Oh come on! There's no need to talk like that! I earn enough for the both of us... we'll survive, we always do. Please Paul, it will be alright."

Paul said, "Well let's not argue about it. It's bad enough as it is."

So they didn't.

Silence came into the room then was expelled when Caitlin said, "I've got a good idea. Let's go out. The circus is only here for one day. You've promised me for a long time that if it came we would go. Well, what do you think?"

"Oh. Okay, fine. There's no point in staying in." She stood up and grabbed his hand.

"Come on then. Who knows? You might even be inspired!"

"Maybe. But I doubt it."

It would have been quicker to have gone by car but they decided to walk because as Caitlin said, "Let's get some country air into our lungs. It'll be good for the both of us."

They left the cottage by the well and followed the path across the fields and through the forests. As usual she was life's little angel, frolicking about, picking flowers and putting them behind her ears.

Paul returned her laughs but it was only pretend. While she was the angel he was the demi-God. The only thing that mattered to him was he himself and his book. Each morning he would return to his word processor, turn it on, and stare at the blank screen. And on those rare occasions that he would actually write something, after a few paragraphs he would press "delete" and erase the whole goddam lot...

..."Paul?"

He fiddled with his earring.

"What?"

She pointed.

"The circus!"

He was dumbstruck because it wasn't what he expected. There was no big top, no giant tent, no grey marquis, no blazing sign that shouted "CIRCUS" painted in bright colours. There weren't even any sounds of animals: like roaring lions or birds squawking.

All there was was a collection of five drab caravans grouped together in a tight circle.

"Is that it?" he asked.   "Caitlin, what sort of circus is this anyhow?"

"Look. There's a sign over the entrance. Let's see what it says."

As they walked closer the letters began to form themselves over the threshold: black letters on a dirty green background. It simply stated,

"CALIGARI'S CIRCUS."

Paul said, "Bit quiet isn't it?"

"They're all inside probably."

The entrance itself was hidden by a blanket, and next to that was a small tin bucket with "ONE POUND" painted on it.

"Are you sure?" he asked.

"Come on! It'll be great. I promise."

They walked down, threw in their money, pulled back the blanket and went inside.

It was really weird because everything was dark. Weird because as far as he could remember there had been no roof on top. He reached out for her hand, found it and grabbed her. The ongoing silence was broken by the phrase: " ...Guests, hurry up. Right, ready? LIGHTS!"

When the lights came on Paul stepped backwards several paces. In front of him was one of the most strangest and scariest things he had ever seen. Gone were the caravans, the grass, the outside world. They were now replaced by an enormous room, like a function hall, decorated in blue, to represent space. The universe. Every now and then there would be little drops of yellow and white, representing the stars. And sometimes there was even the odd planet painted in reds, greens and oranges. He marvelled at how realistic it all looked and for a moment it felt that he was on top of the world.

The room was regimentally fantastic, a hive of activity. There were hundreds of people stumbling idly about, although they seemed to be making their way to the far end of the room where there was a man with a huge box on a wooden platform. But, these people weren't the kind he was used to. Some were, how could he put it? Yes, freaks. Women with beards, men with three legs, girls with two heads, boys with fins.

Past thoughts gone, Paul laughed and turned towards Caitlin. She too was smiling. She let go of his hand and said, "Let the unmasking begin." Paul watched as she took off her jumper, her shoes, her trousers and stood there in her glory. Caitlin wasn't the Caitlin of old. Gone were her human limbs, she now stood proud like a spider.

"What the f... ?"

"Come," she said, offering a limb. "Join with us."

The platform was now illuminated and the rest of the lights in the room went out, making the scenery look even more realistic. The stars and planets seemed to be orbiting around a huge yellow spotlight that covered the way they came in.

The 'people' moved closer to the platform. As Paul and Caitlin walked with them he noticed that now everyone was in their true state, but this glazed look swept the auditorium.

"What happens now?" Paul asked.

"Wait and see."

A huge explosion rocked the hall, smoke poured forth and the small rounded man came into focus.

"Welcome all to Caligari's Circus where Prophets really do speak the truth! The cabinet is waiting. Who will be first?" A spotlight began to move around the audience, revealing faces here and there, flashing faster and faster until it fell on a small old lady. She began to applaud furiously, soon followed by the rest of the people. She leapt up to the platform.

Caligari pressed a button on the side of the wooden cabinet and the old lady stepped back in awe as the door slid open.

"In you go. Liberation."

The old lady stepped hesitantly towards the cabinet, searched the heavens for an answer and crept inside.

Caligari closed the door behind her. A drum roll appeared from nowhere sending strange vibrations throughout the room. The crowd chanted "ZERIONAL FUTURE" and Paul was sure that he saw the sun at the back of the room pulse with the beat.

There was a loud bang and the audience fell quiet. The audience dropped their heads as if in prayer and waited. Smoke poured from the cabinet and the light came back on, and the old lady moved forward.

But as Paul expected she wasn't the same anymore. Gone were the wrinkles, the varicose veins. Gone were the cataracts, her false teeth and plastic hips. Standing in her place was one of the most beautiful butterflies he had ever seen. She opened her wings, tentatively at first, fashioned in a mosaic of colours and rotated her antenna as if searching for something. And what was stranger still was that one minute her body was black, the next white, and the next purple. Caligari moved closer to her, careful not to stand on her wings. He motioned to her to step down and she fluttered off the platform. As she flew through the people she hovered by Paul and whispered into his ear, "Take heed! What is heaven to one is hell to another." He watched as she moved away and disappeared into one of the rings of Saturn.

Attention was now focused back to Caligari and his magical cabinet. He spoke, "We have time for another."

Again the spotlight scanned the crowd. Paul knew that it was to be him. So when the light fell on his head he accepted. With applause ringing throughout his head he made his way onto the stage.

Caligari opened the cabinet and as Paul went inside he turned around and winked at Caitlin. Caligari spoke, "To him that will finally see" and pushed into his hand his drug equipment.

Paul stepped inside.

The cabinet opened and smoke poured out. And a maggot slithered out. And spoke.

"I am the cursed of the Gods."

He raised two stubby furry hands, there in the centre was a bright red eye which winked at the crowd.

"Finally I can see. My new soul feels Winter, Spring, Summer, Autumn. God has loved me and God has cursed me. Our time has come. We must disperse and integrate with the humans. I will call you if God calls me."

While the maggot was talking, Caligari opened his coat and vanished inside. As it wriggled its way off the platform the circus-folk fell to their knees in mock prayer, touched his very fabric of existence and silently laughed.

When the curtain was hauled back he stepped into the harsh sunlight and collapsed onto the grass.

Later.

"How is he doing, Doctor Caligari?"

"I'm sorry, Mrs. Wheaton. He has suffered another relapse. He was caught in the toilets with some talcum powder. We had to put him in the electrocution chamber."

She burst into tears.

"Will he ever get out of here the same man?"

"I doubt it. I'm sorry. He's mad. Quite mad."

She looked at her husband, sitting on the bench eating some leaves, and walked slowly away.

The doctor watched her go. He took off his face and pulled from under his hat a giant starfish.

And said to his patient, "What did you do with my magic dust?" But Paul said nothing, just ate the leaves and stared into the distance.

THE END OF THE LINE

Chug - a - boom.
Chug - a - boom.
Chug - a - boom.

With a whistle and a spurt the ancient black locomotive slowed to a stop into the defunct station. A hiss of sound, a hiss of steam and the train climaxed into the sidings. Another barrage of sound and we were informed that this, a derelict station, was unhappily the end of our journey. To Joe Public this was just another train finishing its run for the night. The smattering steel would be allowed to cool down for a few hours, no more coal to eat nor water to drink - thank God for that.

However this wasn't an old train.

No by Jimminy it wasn't!

It was the thirteen -sixty- one to Nirvana: "The end of the Line."

There was another kiss that followed and the doors opened. This was quietened by the clatter and bang as the exits collided with the hull of the vessel.

And we, the non-paying public, stepped out. We spilled out into the fog, which filled the platform like marbles from a tin. Looking this way and that: deserted souls on a deserted platform; on a macabre platform that led to nowhere.

While we waited impatiently (although time for us was non-existent), the doors closed quietly behind us. And then the train started, driverless and fueless away.

Strange! Because it was the end of the line.

The darkness that before had had us smothered like a new born baby was replaced by a flood of light as several guards appeared. All of them wore pretty little uniforms and stiff caps.

They also had lists.

Of names.

There were to be no commands like:

"WAIT HERE" or "PLEASE BE QUIET" or "WHO WORE THE CLOGS?" because we knew that we should be silent, better not to talk.

The guards formed a circle, with backs to each other, and then they began to read from their lists. When our names were called, we had to follow.

My name was called and I followed my guard (the name GABRIEL was written above his right breast) to a new destination.

But I am afraid I can't tell you where that is. Let us just say that it's further down the platform.

I turned my head and saw that many of the passengers were now leaving the station. Like me, they were hand in hand; one body, one soul. But there were a handful that waited. Some sat down, letting their feet dangle over the edge, while others just stood there and cried.

We walked into the Light, which lay at the exit to the platform, leaving the darkness behind us. We showed our tickets and the gates opened. We walked through. They closed softly.

But like I said, I can't tell you what lay on the other side.

What was that?

The others?

Oh, the OTHERS. Well they crossed over the bridge to the other side of the platform, waiting for the train to take them home.

A train that will never come, because this is the end of the line.

Nothing ever comes this way and if it did, you sure wouldn't want to be on it!

Now, no pushing at the back! Just settle back and wait. It will all be over soon.

And then the adventure begins.